THE NAUGHTIEST UNICORN

AND THE SCHOOL DISCO

PIP BIRD

ILLUSTRATED BY DAVID O'CONNELL

EGMONT

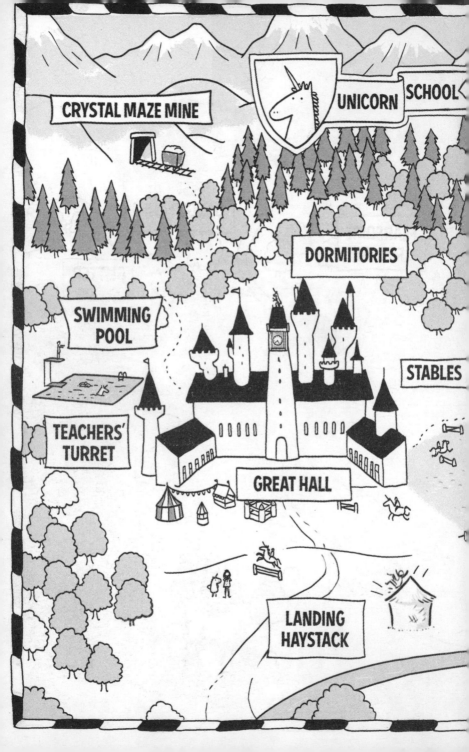

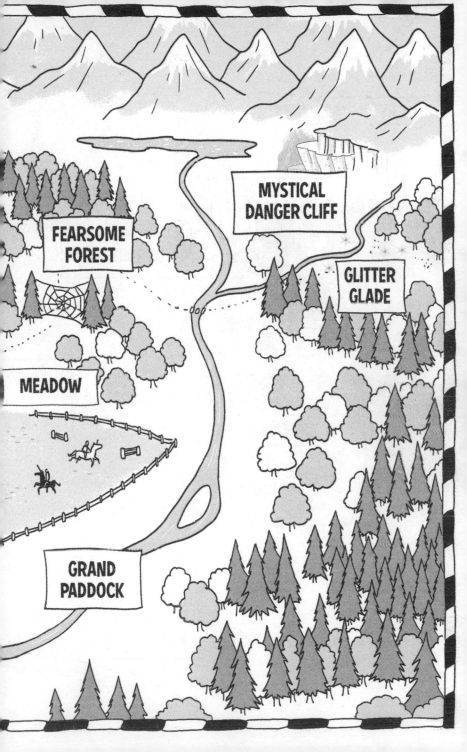

Contents

CHAPTER ONE
Back to Unicorn School!

It was a cloudy Tuesday afternoon and Mira was dancing around the kitchen with her cat, Pickles. Mira's older sister, Rani, rolled her eyes as she finished the after-dinner washing-up (her chore for that week), and flicked water at them as they twirled past the sink.

'Bleurgh!' spluttered Mira as a washing-up bubble landed in her mouth.

Rani dried her hands on a tea towel and snatched Pickles off Mira. 'My turn! Right,

Pickles, you can be my unicorn,' she said. 'I need to practise my moves for the school disco.'

As Rani and Pickles swept past her, Mira had to admit that Rani was an annoyingly good dancer. Rani and her unicorn Angelica were annoyingly good at lots of things. The trophy shelf in their living room was full of all Rani's medals and trophies from winning loads of Unicorn School quests and competitions. Mira had just two medals so far.

Mira and Rani both went to Unicorn School.

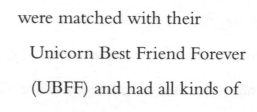

It was a magical place where pupils were matched with their Unicorn Best Friend Forever (UBFF) and had all kinds of

brilliant quests and adventures!

It was almost time to go back to Unicorn School and Mira was BEYOND EXCITED to see her UBFF Dave. He wasn't exactly how she'd imagined her perfect unicorn to be . . . he could be a bit naughty. And greedy. And he fell asleep in all of their lessons. But they had so much fun together. And the disco was going to be the most fun EVER. She couldn't imagine anything better in the entire world than spinning round the dancefloor with Dave!

∪∪∪

Later that night Mira lay in bed, too excited to sleep. She took out her diary from her bedside table and started thinking about all of the awesome things she was going to do with Dave. *And* with Darcy and Raheem – her two human best friends at Unicorn School.

Going on AMAZING quests

Disco with my BFFs

Midnight feasts in the Class Red dormitory

And BEST OF ALL... DAVE MY UBFF!!!!

Thinking about Dave made Mira smile. He always made everything super fun, often in unexpected ways. Sure, he sometimes had to be bribed with snacks to do things. And sometimes he caused a teeny, tiny bit of havoc. *And* he held the Unicorn School record for farting in class. But he didn't *mean* to be naughty. Dave was Mira's UBFF and she loved him.

Mira tucked her diary back in the drawer and fell asleep.

◡◡◡

Mum usually took Mira and Rani to the Magic Portal where they could travel to Unicorn School – but today Dad was driving them and they had to explain *everything* to him. He even nearly forgot to take them to the supermarket to buy treats for their unicorns! (Most unicorns liked carrots and hay, but Dave liked doughnuts best of all.)

'Stop, Dad!' yelled Mira. They were about to drive right past the Magic Portal in the leisure centre car park! Dad made an emergency stop as Mira hung out of the car, waving to her friend Raheem.

Rani refused to be seen dead (her words) with Mira at Unicorn School, so Mira had arranged to go through the portal with Raheem. He was just finishing the ten Rules of Safety song with his dad, but did wave back.

Dad was under strict instructions to take a picture of them before they went through the portal. Rani would only pose for a fraction of a second, but the photo of the back of her head would have to do.

'Bye, Dad!' Mira blew him a kiss through the car window and made sure she had her bag of unicorn treats. 'Ready, Raheem? Why have you got your eyes closed?'

'I always feel sick going through the portal,' Raheem said. 'So I'm doing my calming breathing.'

Mira grabbed his hand and pulled them both through the bushes. No matter how many times

she went through the portal, it never stopped
being absolutely completely magical.

First, her toes started to tingle, then her legs
and arms, and then rainbow light burst all around
them and they were WHOOSHING through
the air before landing with a soft *thump* on the
landing haystack in the middle of the Grand
Paddock at Unicorn School.

'Wow,' breathed Mira as she looked around.
It was autumn and all the leaves in the Fearsome
Forest were turning gorgeous shades of red and
gold. Children were arriving in a steady stream
on the landing haystack and running to find their
UBFFs. The unicorns were grazing and playing in
the paddocks and fields around Unicorn School.

Mira could see their breath puffing in the chilly air as she looked around for Dave.

'Ta-daaaa!' a voice sang out behind them on the haystack. Their friend Darcy launched off the haystack and did a spectacular spin in her wheelchair, ending with her arms in the air.

'Did you miss me?'

Mira laughed and ran over for a hug. 'Of course I missed you. That was awesome!'

Darcy flicked her fluffy blonde hair back over her shoulder. 'I know,' she said. 'I've been practising my moves for the disco. I started a feet-and-wheels dance troop at my other school, because I was kicked off the Murderball team. They said I was too aggressive or something. Anyway, dance is WAY more my thing.'

'What's Murderball?' asked Raheem cautiously.

'It's like rugby but in wheelchairs. And more dangerous,' Darcy replied, looking around for her unicorn, Star.

Raheem looked a little bit lost for words.

'Shall we go and find our unicorns?' he said.

Star and Brave were grazing in the Grand Paddock and cantered over as soon as they spotted Darcy and Raheem. Mira couldn't see Dave.

'Is that him?' asked Darcy, pointing to a giant pile of straw by the side of the fence. Some of the Unicorn School teachers were standing around it, poking something on the top of the straw pile with a stick. Mira looked closer and saw that it was a small unicorn curled up, fast asleep.

'Wake up!' yelled the PE teacher, Miss Hind.

'How is he still asleep?' muttered another teacher, shaking his head.

'He's been up there for sixteen hours!'

said their class teacher, Miss Glitterhorn.

Dave farted loudly in his sleep.

Mira gave a huge smile. *There* was her UBFF.

And she knew JUST how to wake him up!

Mira reached into her pocket. 'Dave!' she called. 'I've got a super special treat for you!' Mira pulled out a strawberry lace and waved it in the air.

Up on the straw pile she was sure she could see Dave's nostrils twitching. Then he gave a loud snort, and sat bolt upright. His ears pricked up, his nose twitched and he looked down at Mira.

Dave launched himself off the top of the straw, bounced off Miss Hind's head and landed in a heap just in front of Mira. Miss Hind muttered crossly to herself but the other teachers just seemed relieved that Dave was finally awake.

Dave snaffled the strawberry lace and licked Mira's face. She giggled and pulled another strawberry lace out of her pocket.

Dave slurped up the treat, then farted happily. Just then the school bell rang, calling the pupils and unicorns inside. It was time for Unicorn School to begin!

CHAPTER TWO
The School Disco Committee

Madame Shetland, the Unicorn School head teacher, waited as everyone gathered in the hall.

'Welcome back to Unicorn School, my dear pupils, unicorns and teachers,' said Madame Shetland. 'Today, I have two very special announcements. Firstly, this week Class Red have a very important quest. Pupils will be travelling to the Crystal Maze Mine to search for Warming Crystals. These crystals heat the school and keep us all warm as the weather turns colder.'

Mira's classmates in Class Red started chatting excitedly. It took three teachers to shush them. Mira high-fived Darcy, who whispered loudly, 'Great, but when can we talk about the disco?'

'And secondly,' continued Madame Shetland, raising her voice over the noise, 'as you know, we will also have a disco. This will take place in three days' time.'

Whoops and squeals of excitement echoed around the hall. Mira grinned happily. A disco AND a super important quest. Amazing!

Two loud taps came over the loudspeakers. Everyone stopped and looked around, wondering what was going on. Darcy had wheeled up to Madame Shetland's podium and taken hold of the microphone.

'Attention please! My fellow students, unicorns, and teachers,' Darcy said. Madame Shetland looked confused and Miss Glitterhorn hurried up to the podium to stop her.

'I have an announcement to make!' Darcy continued. 'I would like to volunteer as Chief Organiser of the School Disco Committee. Together, we can make this a super sensational school disco!'

The pupils burst into applause, as Miss Glitterhorn made it to the podium. 'Err, is there a Disco Committee?' Miss Glitterhorn asked Madame Shetland, who shrugged.

'No . . .' she said thoughtfully, 'but why not? Might make things easier for us teachers. That's enough now, Darcy, no need to start a Mexican wave.'

'Shall I just do a stage dive and crowd surf to finish?' Darcy asked the head teacher.

'No, thank you, Darcy.' Madame Shetland paused for a moment to think. 'Each class shall look after

one part of the disco preparations. Darcy, you
may oversee all the arrangements.'

As the morning bell rang for lessons, Mira led
Dave out of the hall to their classroom and gave
him a massive hug. It was so brilliant that Darcy
was going to be Chief Organiser of the disco . . .
even if it was a job she'd just made up!

∪∪∪

Darcy didn't waste any time. At morning break,
she gathered the first meeting of the Super
Sensational School Disco Committee in the gym.
Madame Shetland and Miss Glitterhorn had
decided that Class Red would select the music
and be in charge of the lighting, and Darcy had
decided she would create a super-awesome first

dance to get the party started!

Mira and Dave were rushing to the meeting because they were a bit late – they'd had to stop for snacks on the way. They passed Jake and his unicorn, Pegasus, doing some cool break-dancing moves down the hallway.

'Let's try that, Dave,' Mira said, attempting a wiggle that started in her head and went down to her feet.

Dave watched her, and then did a massive burp.

'We can work on your moves,' Mira said, pushing the door open.

Inside the gym, Darcy and Star had pushed all the crash mats and benches to the side except for one piece of gym equipment which Darcy sat behind like a desk. Rainbow-coloured climbing ropes hung from the ceiling behind her like a curtain. Darcy's unicorn Star counted the children and unicorns coming in to the gym and showed them where to sit.

Darcy banged on her makeshift table and

signalled for quiet. Freya whispered, 'Where did she get the hammer?'

'It's called a gavel,' said Raheem.

Mia realised that Darcy was taking the role of Chief Organiser *very* seriously.

'Order, order!' called Darcy. 'I declare the first meeting of the Super Sensational School Disco Committee open!' She paused. 'You may applaud.'

Everyone quickly started clapping.

'You're welcome,' Darcy continued. 'The first thing we have to do is – yes, Jake?'

Jake was standing up with his hand raised. 'How come YOU'RE disco leader? I think we should have a vote on who should be in charge.'

Everyone groaned. Jake ALWAYS wanted to be leader!

'Sit down, Jake, this isn't a quest,' called Freya.

Jake went red and started to talk back, but

Darcy just spoke over him. 'As I was saying!

The first order of business is . . . the theme for

the disco. Star – are you taking minutes?'

Star blushed and trotted back to Darcy. She took out a notepad and a sparkly gel pen.

Zara from Class Indigo put up her hand. 'What about unicorns from history as a theme?' he said.

'That's fun!' said Mira. 'Ooh! Or what about fireworks? Or cats?'

'Those are . . . ideas,' said Darcy. '*I* was thinking – Star, drum roll, please – glitter fever!' Darcy flung her arms out in a big 'ta-da' move.

'What about under the sea?' said Seb.

Then children started shouting out their ideas all at once:

'Stars!'

'Space!'

'SLOTHS!' Everyone turned to Flo, Freya's

twin sister, and she shrugged. 'What? I like sloths.'

Darcy shook her head. 'Stop just saying things that begin with "S"!' She tried to continue but was interrupted by more theme ideas.

'Unicycles!'

'Umbrellas!'

'Uranium!'

Darcy banged her gavel and looked cross. 'Now you're just saying things that begin with "U". STOP IT, we're having a vote!'

Everyone sat back down and Darcy smiled. Mira thought it looked a little forced. Darcy continued. 'Right, we'll have a vote on the top three ideas. Everybody close your eyes and raise your hand or hoof for the theme you like best. Star will count the votes. Close your eyes now!'

Darcy called out the three theme ideas in order: space, umbrellas and glitter fever. Mira frowned as she realised that Darcy had decided which three ideas were the best.

'Do you think she's taking this a bit too seriously?' Mira whispered to Raheem, opening one eye.

Raheem shrugged and kept his eyes tightly shut.

'Keep those hands up, please!' said Darcy sternly.

Mira thought Star was taking a long time to count the votes. She realised that Star was frantically crossing out on her notepad then looking up to count the raised hands and hoofs again. Mira felt bad for the unicorn. She found counting hard, too, especially under pressure. Sometimes Mira skipped right from 29 to 40 if she wasn't thinking carefully.

Dave grunted and shuffled out of the line. Mira guessed he was hungry.

Darcy banged her gavel again and told everyone to open their eyes. Mira could see Dave sniffing around near Darcy. He's probably searching for snacks, thought Mira.

'I am thrilled to announce,' said Darcy, 'that the winner by LOADS of votes is . . . GLITTER FEVER!'

Raheem and Mira clapped and a few other pupils joined in too. No one looked quite as excited as Darcy. Freya whispered to Mira, 'That was totally a fix. Darcy just made up the result.'

Mira frowned. She did agree with Freya that the vote didn't quite seem fair . . . but she knew Darcy just wanted every part of the disco to be perfect, and she certainly had lots of brilliant ideas!

Just then there was a huge crash behind Darcy. Raheem screamed and hid behind his chair, and the other pupils and unicorns started running around in a panic. When the dust settled, Mira saw Dave, thoughtfully chewing the red climbing rope, with the other ropes in a heap all over

Darcy's desk. Darcy sat crossly amongst the

rubble, covered in dust.

Mira ran over to see if her friend was okay.

Darcy was bright red in the face and did not look happy.

'Darcy, I'm so sorry!' Mira said. 'I think Dave thought the red climbing rope was a giant strawberry lace.'

'It's fine!' said Darcy, coughing up some dust. Star trotted around, picking up the disco notes, which had fallen all over the floor.

Mira kept asking if Darcy was okay as they cleared up and Darcy kept saying she was fine, but Mira was sure she heard Darcy muttering 'nightmare unicorn' and 'super greedy'.

The bell rang to end morning break and Darcy and Star left the gym quickly, with Darcy still muttering under her breath.

Dave nudged Mira's elbow. She pulled out a real strawberry lace from her pocket for him and he gave a happy fart.

CHAPTER THREE
Glitter Fever...

Later that day, after lunch, it was time for PE.

Miss Hind, the PE teacher, blew her whistle and called Class Red together. Mira headed to the back of the group, tugging Dave along with her.

'Now, Class Red, we have a change of lesson plan today,' barked Miss Hind. 'As you know, Class Red will be opening the school disco with a special dance routine, which Darcy has created. I am thrilled to be helping you learn your special dance.' (Mira couldn't help thinking that Miss

Hind didn't look very thrilled.)

Miss Hind pressed play on the speaker. 'Here
is the song you will be dancing to, written by
none other than . . . Darcy. It's called *Glitter Fever's
Gonna Get You*.'

The room suddenly filled with very loud
music. Raheem clamped his hands over his ears
and squeezed his eyes shut. Darcy whooped
and started spinning around in circles in her
wheelchair, rainbow wheel rims flashing
as she sang along. Flo and her unicorn ran round
and round the hall. Even Dave woke up from
his nap and flicked his ears back and forth to the
music as it filled the air.

Mira felt a little thrill as she tapped her feet.

Disco dancing

Unicorns prancing

Hooves in the air

Like you just don't care

Stable strutting

Popping and tutting

Everybody get down

Glitter fever is coming to town!

Mira couldn't believe Darcy had written a whole song! She felt really proud of her friend and she couldn't wait to learn the dance routine.

On Mira's very first trip to Unicorn School

Dave had surprised her by being completely brilliant at prancing. Maybe, just maybe, Dave would also be great at dancing. Maybe they'd get a dancing medal at the disco! After all, dancing was a bit like prancing but to music . . .

Raheem nudged Mira with his elbow and whispered. 'What's . . . glitter fever?'

'What?' Mira whispered back.

'In the song – glitter fever. What is it?' Raheem looked even more worried than usual.

Darcy overheard and jumped in. 'Nobody knows, Raheem.' She flicked her hair. 'But it's going to get you and everyone else!'

'That's what I'm worried about,' Raheem replied.

'Mira and Raheem!' shouted Miss Hind. 'Stop chatting and get in line with your unicorns.'

The children and unicorns were soon standing in two lines, one behind the other. Miss Hind started teaching the dance. 'OK, *five, six, seven, eight*, and children take two steps to the right, unicorns two steps left, turn and look at your partner – snap! Two steps the other way, turn and – snap! And then children turn to face your unicorn, hold hands and hooves and sliiiiiiide . . .'

Star gave a snort as Dave trod on her hoof.

Pegasus glared as Dave spun around on his tummy in a circle, making Mira laugh loudly.

'Come *on* Dave!' snapped Darcy. 'That's not one of the dance moves!'

Mira frowned. 'It's Dave's first time, Darcy. We'll get it in the end. Not all of the unicorns can do different things with their front and back legs.'

Miss Hind called Darcy and Star up to the front to demonstrate the next move.

The next move was actually a long series of moves. They all tried to follow Darcy and Star, but it was a struggle. Two unicorns fell over.

'It's quite complicated,' said Mira, poking herself in the eye.

'Don't worry, it's just armography,' said Darcy. Jake and his unicorn, Pegasus, got the hang of it straightaway, and looked really cool. Freya had a fit of giggles when she accidentally hit herself in the nose. Flo and her unicorn, Sparkles, looked like they might cry because they couldn't do it.

Raheem and Brave just looked lost.

Dave really was trying hard to get it right.
But as he and Mira tried the moves, his legs got
tangled and, very slowly, he toppled over and
caused all of the other unicorns to tumble down.

Darcy glared at them both. 'Seriously! Stop messing around!'

'We're not messing around!' Mira shouted back.

Freya put her hands on her hips. 'Darcy, none of us have ever done this before. You and Star were rehearsing all lunchtime, so you've had a headstart.'

'Some of us are just naturally talented actually!' said Darcy, as Star's tummy rumbled. She looked embarrassed and hid behind Darcy's wheelchair.

Miss Hind blew her whistle. 'That's enough dancing for now, class. Let's move on to ab work.'

'Ab . . . a-a-ab work?' stammered Raheem.

'Yes,' said Miss Hind. 'A strong core is essential for a dancer's posture.'

CHAPTER FOUR
Quest Countdown

At dinnertime, when Mira and Dave sat down
at the Class Red dinner table, Star had her
muzzle on the table and was snoring. Dave gave
her a nudge. She woke up with a snort.

'Is she okay?' asked Freya through a mouthful
of mashed potato.

'She's fine,' said Darcy. 'Star, we have lots to do.
Don't get lazy like Dave.'

'Darcy! That's not nice,' said Raheem.

Dave did not seem to be offended. Very calmly,
he took a big bite out of Darcy's clipboard.

'Mira!' Darcy shrieked. 'Those are my super important party planning notes. Make him STOP!'

Seb arrived and plonked his dinner tray down in between Darcy and Dave. 'Can I draw some posters for the disco? Firework and I had some ideas for the glitter fever theme.'

Darcy wiped Dave's slobber off the clipboard

with her sleeve. 'That sounds great, Seb, thank you. Star and I have already started working on some designs . . . but perhaps you can colour them in?'

Mira frowned. Why was Darcy speaking so weirdly . . . like a teacher or a parent?

'Ooh, ooh!' Flo put up her hand. 'Can Sparkles and I be on the Welcoming Committee? We thought it would be lovely to sprinkle glitter confetti over people as they walk in to the disco.'

'Hmmn, that might be nice,' said Darcy thoughtfully. 'I mean it's supposed to be Class Yellow's job but I'm sure we can help them. As long as the glitter confetti is gold and matches the rest of the colour scheme.'

'Pegasus and I can be in charge of the food,' said Jake. 'We like baking.'

Darcy smiled. 'Happy for you to help. Just make sure you follow the recipes carefully. Star, are you taking notes on all this?'

Mira narrowed her eyes. Darcy was becoming disco obsessed and she didn't even sound like herself any more. What was going on?

∪ ∪ ∪

Next morning, the first lesson was Science. Miss Glitterhorn clapped to start the class, just as Jake and Pegasus jogged in.

'Sorry, miss, we were doing some extra training for the quest this afternoon,' said Jake, panting.

Mira smiled to herself. The thought of the quest made her tummy flutter. Quests were Mira's absolute favourite thing!

Darcy raised her hand. 'Speaking of the quest, Miss Glitterhorn, don't you think Class Red are too young for such an important task? I mean, maybe we should all stay behind and work on the disco?'

'Can we have one lesson that's NOT about the disco?' Mira said, frowning at Darcy. 'That's all you're interested in at the moment!'

Miss Glitterhorn glared at the two of them. 'Now, now, girls. Class Red are perfect for this quest. We need to collect Warming Crystals before winter comes to the land. Warming Crystals form in small, honeycomb pockets in the walls of the Crystal Cave Mine. Since you're the youngest and smallest, your hands are the perfect size to fit into the holes and collect the crystals.'

Miss Glitterhorn drew a series of diagrams on the white board demonstrating how the crystals should be carefully removed from the cavern wall, with each human and unicorn pair working together to release the crystal. Everyone carefully took notes, apart from Dave who was noisily eating crisps and Darcy who was listening to music and sketching disco outfits in her notebook.

'Now!' their teacher continued. 'Today we are also learning about the reflective properties of glitter and crystals! One person from each

pair please come up to collect the mirrors and torches.'

Darcy and Mira were *meant* to be working together. But Darcy just kept whispering to Star and making her write down things about the disco. So Mira had to go up and get the mirror and the torch.

Miss Glitterhorn explained how light bounced off shiny surfaces and made things sparkle. Flo was sticking little squares of mirror to Sparkles' horn to make it shine like a crystal. Dave thought that was funny and spiked a mirror tile on the end of his horn. As he turned to show Mira, the morning sunlight caught on the mirror and shone directly into Darcy's eyes.

'Argh!' she yelled. 'Dave's blinded me! I can't see anyth— OH! I've had a BRILLIANT IDEA!'

Miss Glitterhorn clapped in delight. 'About reflection?'

'No, well, sort of . . .' Darcy stopped herself. 'Um, when is the quest again?'

'After lunch, Darcy. Now, what was your brilliant idea?'

'Oh, nothing, I forgot.' Darcy smiled a small and very secret smile. As Mira helped Dave get the mirror off his horn, she wondered what Darcy was up to. She was sure it would have something to do with the disco . . .

∪∪∪

After lunch it was time for the the quest! Not only were quests Mira's favourite thing about Unicorn School BUT there was always the chance of getting a medal. Mira was so excited that she was hopping from foot to foot. Dave started hopping too, then trod on Mira's toe.

Class Red lined up outside the unicorn stables. Colin the caretaker was handing out boiler suits and helmets with headlamps for Class Red pupils and hornlamps for the unicorns. The children changed into their safety gear and helped glitter-shoe their unicorns. Glitter helped to protect the unicorns and they *always* put glitter on their hooves before a quest.

Raheem asked Colin if the unicorns needed

helmets too, for safety. Colin said no, unicorn skulls were much stronger than children's and that they were so hard they could probably even win a headbutting contest with a rhinoceros. Raheem looked a bit pale and asked if it was likely they might see a rhinoceros in the mine. Colin said no and carried on checking everyone's unicorns had been glitter-shoed.

Miss Hind blew her whistle and glared at the class. 'Right! Everyone please mount your unicorns and follow me. I want a nice, clean quest with no funny business or you can FORGET about going to the school disco. Oh, and I've decided that your quest leader will be Jake.'

Jake's 'YES!' was so loud that Sparkles cantered off in fright. Flo went to fetch her and a few minutes later they all set off into the forest.

Raheem had insisted that Brave wear a helmet, even though he did NOT look happy about it.

But, finally, they were on their quest! Mira didn't even mind that Jake was quest leader. She threw Dave a doughnut and he happily trotted after it, giving Mira a little bottom wiggle to say thanks.

Maybe, just this once, Mira would get to have a normal, completely brilliant quest. She couldn't wait to get started!

CHAPTER FIVE
The Crystal Maze Mine

The entrance to the Crystal Maze Mine was in
a rough, grey cliff edge at the other side of the
Fearsome Forest. Mira was surprised to see a
railway track in front of the mine.

'We're getting a TRAIN?' said Raheem,
his eyes wide. 'I thought it was just a cave!'

How deep underground is it?'

'We're going to the centre of the Earth!' sang Flo as she trotted past with Sparkles.

'The centre of the Earth?' repeated Raheem, his eyes widening. 'What if we never get out?!'

Miss Hind blew her whistle as Mira comforted Raheem. 'Right, Class Red, please come and get one special collection box each. These are *very* high-tech and very precious. You will each fill all six spaces with a Warming Crystal, and no more! We need this exact number of Warming Crystals to heat the school and unicorns through the winter. We must only collect what we truly need, no more and nothing else. Remember Unicorn School Rule number 73: Leave the Forest As You Find It.'

Jake helped hand out the special collection boxes, which had six little holes and a lid.

'Are these . . . egg boxes?' asked Seb. 'I thought you said they were high-tech.'

'No talking back!' shouted Miss Hind. 'Yes, they were inspired by egg boxes – a perfect piece of design. Now, you will each get into the railway carts, children in front to steer, unicorns in the back. Keep all arms, legs and unicorns inside the cart at all times! The way to the Warming Crystal Cavern is VERY WELL SIGNPOSTED. Do NOT go off the rickety railway tracks, and DO NOT GO anywhere other than the Warming Crystal Cavern. Go straight there and come straight back once you have filled your egg boxes. I mean, special collection boxes. Understood?'

'Understood!' Class Red shouted back at Miss Hind.

'Why is it called the *rickety* railway track?' whispered Raheem.

Before anyone had time to answer, the class raced to the railway carts, fighting to get into the front carriages.

'Remember, children please sit in the front of the railway carts. Jake will be driving in the front cart and steering and all the carts are attached to each other, so everyone else should be

able to sit back and enjoy the ride.'

Raheem buckled himself and Brave into their cart, looking pretty queasy. Mira jumped in the cart next to him and lured Dave into the back with a chocolate finger.

Miss Hind told them all to switch on their headlamps and waved them off into the mine. As Mira was near the back, she could see Miss Hind watching a unicorn wrestling match on her phone even before the train was completely in the tunnel.

Everything went dark. Raheem whimpered a little. Mira did think this quest seemed a little bit dangerous. It was so exciting!

Jake started leading a teamwork song:

1, 2, 3, 4, together we achieve much more!

5, 6, 7, 8, unicorns are really great!

Mira joined in, and smiled when she could

hear Darcy singing the loudest of all. Darcy loved singing.

Dave was scratching at his hornlamp with a front hoof. The light flickered on and off, bouncing against the tunnel walls. Brave hiccupped.

'Dave, can you stop that?' asked Raheem.

Mira turned around. 'I think his hornlamp is really uncomfortable,' she said.

'It's making Brave trainsick.'

Brave hiccupped again.

Mira fed Dave another treat to stop him from fidgeting. Thanks to the light coming from the headlights and hornlights, Mira could see that there were lots of tunnels and railway tracks

leading off from their tunnel. As they trundled down the track, they saw little bits of crystals and precious gemstones all around, glinting in the walls and the roof. They passed a sign for the 'Emerald Cave' and Mira saw an incredible green glow from the tunnel.

'Raheem, I think we're nearly at the Glitter Slime Gorge!' Mira said eagerly.

Raheem just gulped but there were 'oohs'

from the rest of Class Red as they caught sight
of the spectacularly sparkly cliff edge through
an opening in the walls.

There was a huge SLURP sound and a glitter boulder popped out from the top of the gorge, slipping down the cliff with a trail of oozing sparkly slime. Mira thought she saw someone lean out of a cart up ahead, and Raheem yelped, 'SAFETY FIRST! Stay inside the carts!'

The railway carts turned another corner and down a small slope and then stopped. Jake – who was clutching a map of the Crystal Maze Mine – announced that they had arrived at the Warming Crystal Cavern.

The unicorns and their humans climbed out of the tunnel (Dave had fallen asleep during the journey and Flo had to help Mira lift him out of the cart, still snoring loudly). It got warmer as they left the tunnel and turned into the cavern. It was quite dark and Mira was glad she was wearing her headlamp. Other Class Red pairs had already started collecting crystals so Mira woke up Dave and hurried to find an empty section of wall.

Mira remembered from the Science class how to feel along the wall for a soft section, then get Dave to poke a hole in the crystal crust with his horn. She scooped out dirt from the hole and reached in until her fingers felt something smooth and round. With a bit more digging, she just about got her fingers round the crystal. It felt warm in her hand. Gently, she pulled it out and gasped. In response, Dave gave a huge belch.

The Warming Crystal was the size of a large marble, and it started to swirl all kinds of beautiful colours, from green to blue and purple, just like the amazing rainbow lights from the last quest Mira had been on.

She carefully popped the crystal in the special collection box.

Mira worked quickly to fill her box with more crystals and gave Dave a little hug. This was fun! Someone started to sing the teamwork song again and Mira joined in, but realised it sounded quieter than before. Something was missing . . .

Mira looked around the Cavern. Then she realised. It wasn't something missing, it was some*one*. Darcy had disappeared!

CHAPTER SIX
Glitter Slime Gorge

Mira panicked. Where could Darcy *be*?

She thought fast. Dragging Dave behind her, she scuttled over to Raheem and Brave.

'Raheem,' she hissed. 'Darcy's missing!'

Raheem looked around. 'Uh-oh,' he said. 'And her railway cart's gone, too.'

'Come on! We've got to go and find her. She could be in trouble!'

Raheem looked scared. 'But . . . but we're not supposed to go anywhere outside this cavern!'

'Raheem we HAVE to find Darcy!' said

Mira firmly. 'She could be ANYWHERE. And she's our friend. We have to find her and bring her back safely.'

Raheem sighed nervously. 'Okay fine, but shouldn't we at least tell Jake where we're going?'

'NO! We've got to do this secretly. Follow me,' whispered Mira.

They snuck off to the last railway cart and put their egg boxes full of Warming Crystals carefully inside. Luckily, the other Class Red pupils and unicorns were distracted by the gathering of the crystals. Mira unhooked the cart from the one in front and put her last doughnut on the edge of the cart. Dave shunted forwards to gobble it up and set the cart trundling off down

the railway track. Mira pushed Raheem and the two unicorns inside while it was moving, and then jumped in herself.

'How . . . how do you know which way we're going?' Raheem asked in a trembly voice.

'I don't,' said Mira.

'What?!'

'I figured you would have memorised the map,' Mira said.

'Oh, right,' said Raheem. 'Yes, I have. So, where do you want to look first?'

They decided to retrace their steps.

They poked their heads into the Glorious Opal Shaft, but Darcy wasn't there. Then they checked in the Emerald Cave, but there was no sign of her there either. Back in the main tunnel, two large glittery boulders rolled past them. They shivered. Then Mira remembered Darcy's love of glitter . . . after all she had chosen the disco theme glitter fever AND written the song *Glitter Fever's Gonna*

Get You. Suddenly Mira knew JUST where Darcy would be. 'The Glitter Slime Gorge!' she shrieked, making Raheem jump.

Raheem directed Mira back to the cliff, and then reached over suddenly to pull the brake. Everyone jerked forwards and Brave groaned. Dave, on the other hand, was whinnying joyfully. He seemed to really like the railway, when he could stay awake.

Raheem pointed straight ahead. Mira looked at the track which sloped into a steep, steep spiral to the bottom of the Glitter Slime Gorge.

'Maybe she's not –' began Raheem, just as they heard someone singing *Glitter Fever's Gonna Get You* at the bottom of the cliff.

'If that's not Darcy, then Dave's not my unicorn,' said Mira, and flipped off the brake, sending them whizzing down the track like a rollercoaster.

'WweEEEeeEE,' cried Mira.

'AAArrgggHH,' shrieked Raheem.

'BLEeeugHH,' groaned Brave.

'BBRrrrrrRRRR,' Dave snorted happily, his muzzle hanging over the side of the railway cart, tongue waggling in the rush of air.

THUMP!

They came came to a sudden stop by bumping into another cart at the bottom of the gorge. They all shivered. It really was chilly down here.

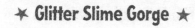

'Hooves in the air, like you just don't care!
Glitter fever is comin' to town!'

Raheem and Mira clambered out of the cart
and turned a corner to see Darcy riding Star,
singing happily and clutching two giant Sticky
Glitter boulders. Her eyes had a wild look in
them. Star was rolling a couple more glitter
boulders along the floor towards the carts with
her hooves.

'She looks a bit . . . strange,' Mira whispered
to Raheem.

Raheem nodded wisely. 'She's got glitter fever.'

Mira thought for a moment and then turned
sideways and held out her hands in front of her,
fingers spread. She edged towards Darcy, who

was still singing very loudly and didn't seem to have noticed them.

'What are you doing?' asked Raheem.

'I saw this on a TV programme about bears,' replied Mira. 'When they're worked up, you have to approach with great caution.'

Then she said in a soothing voice, 'Darcy, it's okay, you're not going to be in trouble, just put down the glitter boulder and come back with us.'

'NO!' said Darcy with wide eyes and a huge smile. 'Can't you see? A Sticky Glitter boulder is just what the disco needs! This Sticky Glitter boulder will make the most amazing glitterball. We'll hang it up, and shine lights on it and it will be EPIC! Woohoo!'

Star whinnied in agreement.

'Mira's right, Darcy,' said Raheem. 'We're not supposed to be here, and we're not supposed to take anything other than the Warming Crystals out of the mine. Remember School Rule 73: Leave the Forest As You Find It?'

'Yes, Raheem. Firstly, we are not technically *in* the forest. And secondly, Miss Hind said "only take what you need". And we NEED this glitterball!' Star was now nudging the boulders towards the traintrack and trying to roll them up into the cart.

'Darcy, NO!' Mira gave up using her soothing voice. Darcy was being totally selfish! 'We'll ALL get into so much trouble! Leave the Sticky Glitter boulders here and let's just get back to the quest.' Mira rolled Star's boulder away from the tracks.

'GIVE THOSE BACK!' shouted Darcy. 'The disco needs them!'

'No, we NEED to get back to the quest! The disco really doesn't matter THAT much,'

Mira yelled back.

'It DOES matter!'

Darcy kept tight hold of the Sticky Glitter
boulders. 'Raheem, you can tell Mira that I'm no
longer speaking to her.'

Mira crossed her arms and turned to Raheem.
'You can tell Darcy that *I'm* not speaking to *her*.'

'Well, you can tell Mira that I wouldn't have
to stop speaking to her if her unicorn hadn't
destroyed my meeting, almost blinded me AND
eaten my disco notes!'

Mira glared at Darcy. 'Well, you can tell Darcy
that if she wasn't being so incredibly annoying
about the disco, maybe Dave wouldn't have felt
the need to be SO NAUGHTY!'

As Mira and Darcy carried on yelling at each other, Raheem looked back and forth at his friends, his head moving from side to side.

'STOP YELLING!' he finally shouted, accidentally knocking one of the Sticky Glitter boulders out of Darcy's hands so that it splattered on the floor in an oozy lump of slime.

CHAPTER SEVEN
To the Rescue!

Looking a bit shocked, Darcy let the other
Sticky Glitter boulder roll down on to the floor.
She wiped her nose on her sleeve.

'Look,' she said, sniffing. 'I'm not the best at
anything at Unicorn School. Raheem, you're
so clever and Mira you always manage to get
medals despite Dave being, you know, different.
But I LOVE dancing and I just wanted to show
everyone what a good job I could do with the
disco. Maybe I did get a bit carried away.'

Mira suddenly felt sorry for her friend.

'Darcy, you're doing an amazing job, you're a brilliant disco leader! But if we don't get back to the group soon, Miss Hind will find out you went missing and then *no one* will get to enjoy the disco.' Mira paused for a moment and looked at Darcy's sad face as she stroked a glitter boulder. 'Listen, I know we're not allowed to take anything from the mine, but this Sticky Glitter really is awesome. Maybe you could just take back a few bits that have already broken off?'

Darcy nodded hard. 'I mean,' she said, 'when you think about it, really we're just rescuing it!' She turned to Dave. 'Dave, I'm sorry I snapped at you. I didn't mean it!'

Dave, who was rummaging around in the back

of the cart, turned and shrugged.

'Can we please just get a move on and head back to the rest of the class?' asked Raheem. He was jiggling nervously from foot to foot.

Darcy and Mira agreed and they quickly got back in the carts.

No one moved.

'Uh-oh,' said Raheem, his eyes widening.

'What?' Darcy and Mira replied at the same time.

'We're stuck at the bottom of a steep hill,' Raheem shrieked. 'We can't get back up the rickety railway spiral!'

'There must be a way, we've just got to think positive,' said Darcy.

Raheem tried his deep calming breaths.

'No, we've got the two back railway carts.

The front cart is the only one with an engine.

We might be stuck down here forever!'

Brave gave Raheem a hug. Dave gave a sympathetic fart. A colourful cloud appeared behind him. It smelled of marshmallows.

Mira looked at Dave. Had he just farted out a *rainbow cloud*? She shook her head. That was pretty strange but right now she had bigger things to worry about. She *really* didn't want to be stuck in the Glitter Slime Gorge forever!

Dave farted loudly again and this time the cloud was pink. Mira heard a crunching sound. She looked at Dave, then at her egg box. Two crystals were missing. She narrowed her eyes. 'Dave! Did you eat the Warming Crystals?'

Dave stopped chewing, then let out another noisy fart cloud, a massive one this time.

The cart shot forwards a little way and he jumped in surprise at its power.

'Dave, eating the crystals is genuinely a really naughty thing to do!' said Darcy, admiringly.

'Dave, you're actually a genius!' said Mira. 'Quick, finish the crystals.' Before her friends could object, she handed Dave the rest of the egg box, and shoved his bottom out the back of the cart.

Dave gobbled up the crystals, swallowed and licked his lips.

Then, with an almighty blast and an extra-large cloud, Dave did an enormous rainbow fart and WHOOOSH! The railway carts launched back up the train tracks.

'WHEEEEEEEEE!' yelled Darcy, with her hands in the air.

'AAAAAAAARGH!' cried Raheem.

'WHOOO HOOOO!' shrieked Mira.

Even Raheem was giddy with excitement
by the time they turned the last spiral corner and
got back up to the main tunnel. He guided the
carts down the tracks to the Warming Crystal
Cavern. Mira couldn't believe they'd made it.
They'd rescued Darcy *and* made it safely back to
the group. Maybe no one had even noticed they
were gone. They could just fill their egg boxes
and finish quickly. And then finish the quest!

'Where have you BEEN?' Jake yelled at them
as soon as they crept into the Warming Crystal
Cavern. His face was a funny colour and he
looked really worried.

'I told you they'd come back,' said Freya. 'It's
cool, come on, time to go.'

'You're going to be in SO MUCH
TROUBLE,' said Jake threateningly.

Seb put a hand on his shoulder. 'Jake, it's
fine. They're here now. Let's just get back to
Miss Hind.'

Jake held up their empty egg boxes from the railway cart. 'It's NOT fine – their special collection boxes are empty! We need to fill every single one. I'm quest leader, remember, I know this stuff!' Jake was really red in the face now.

Darcy rolled her eyes. 'Jake, don't be so dramatic. Let's just hurry up, fill our egg boxes and get back in the carts.'

Jake scowled and told everyone else to start loading up the railway carts.

Mira, Darcy and Raheem headed to an empty cave wall section.

'Thanks Jake!' said Mira brightly, as she started feeling for a Warming Crystal pocket in the wall. 'Darcy, here's one!'

Mira and Darcy grinned at each other.

It felt SO good for everything to be back to normal! Jake rolled his eyes and yelled, 'Just HURRY UP!' then stormed off to boss around the children and unicorns getting back into the railway carts.

∪∪∪

The journey back was very jolly. Even Jake cheered up as he led everyone in a loud rendition of the teamwork song. At last, they saw a little bit of sunlight at the end of the tunnel and soon were out in the forest again.

Miss Hind counted the children as they got out of the carts. '. . . 17, Raheem . . . 18, Darcy – WHAT IS THAT?!'

'What is what, Miss Hind?' said Darcy innocently.

'The glittery thing poking out of your rucksack,' said Miss Hind.

Darcy gasped, opening her bag. 'A glitterball!' she said. 'Oh no! It must have accidentally fallen into my bag.'

Miss Hind narrowed her eyes.

'I mean, I guess it'll look super cool at the disco so it's lucky really . . .' Darcy carried on.

Miss Hind loomed over Darcy. 'That's not a "glitterball", Darcy, it's Sticky Glitter from the Glitter Slime Gorge. You should not have been anywhere near that gorge! The quest was very clear, Darcy: *only* collect the Warming Crystals and come straight back. School Rule number 73: Leave the Forest As You Find It.'

A crowd of their classmates had gathered to see what all the fuss was about, and everyone started ooh-ing and aah-ing at the Sticky Glitter.

Miss Hind looked like she might explode. She picked up the Sticky Glitter and hurled it back into the tunnel. It took her a couple of tries because the glitter was sticking to her hands. It really was very sticky. She turned back to the class. Her face had turned a strange shade of red.

'Class Red, you disobeyed my instructions and MUST be punished. Therefore, none of you will go to the school disco!' shouted Miss Hind.

Class Red gasped.

'But, Miss Hind,' stammered Darcy, 'It was my–'

'SILENCE!' yelled Miss Hind. 'If I hear one more word from any of you then you'll all be in even MORE trouble!'

★ To the Rescue! ★

CHAPTER EIGHT
Disco Disaster

The journey back through the Fearsome Forest
was very quiet. Mira had run out of snacks so
Dave kept veering off the path to try and eat the
sparklebushes. Soon they were way behind the
rest of the class. Mira sighed.

'Oh, Dave, I was so looking forward to the
disco.' Dave snorted in sympathy. 'And I was so
excited about the quest! But now we don't get to
dance together, or win any medals.'

Dave turned his head to try and cheer her up,
but accidentally tipped Mira off into a bush.

He licked her face to apologise.

Mira was brushing leaves off her jumper when she heard someone giggling and saw Flo waiting on the path.

'What's so funny?' Mira asked.

'Oh, I'm just happy,' said Flo. 'I know we can't go to the disco, but wasn't the quest fun? And my boiler suit is so pretty! I'm NEVER going to take it off. And I'm spending time with my BEST friend.' Flo gave Sparkles a big hug.

Mira smiled and hauled herself back up on to Dave. They trotted down the path together. Flo was right. They had done the right thing by rescuing Darcy, even though it had meant they all lost out on going to the disco. As Dave let out a

small colourful fart cloud Mira couldn't help
but smile. Whatever else happened, she still had
her UBFF!

∪ ∪ ∪

Back at the stables, everyone took off their boiler suits and put them in a big washing basket. (Everyone apart from Flo who smuggled hers back to her room.) They led their unicorns into their stalls and groomed them, mane to tail. Mira gave Dave fresh hay in his nosebag and fresh straw for his bed.

Behind her, Mira heard Jake boasting to some of their classmates.

'I can't believe I collected SO MANY crystals. There were actually too many for the boxes so I had to leave most of them behind. One of them was SO HOT it nearly burned my arm off. I basically aced the quest before Darcy ruined it for everyone.'

A few of the children sighed and looked sad.
Mira wanted to stick up for Darcy, but she could
see how disappointed they all were about the
missing out on the disco.

Mira saw that Dave already finished his hay,
so she went out to get him some more and
bumped into Seb coming out of Star's stable.

'Have you seen Darcy?' Seb asked.

'No, why?' said Mira.

'She's missing again. So is Star.'

Mira felt hot and her heart started racing.
Darcy had been very quiet the whole way home.
She obviously felt really bad about making the
whole class miss the disco.

Maybe Darcy had run away with Star into the

forest . . . or maybe she'd gone into hiding . . . or maybe she had gone back home early through the Magic Portal and they'd never see her again? Mira had only just made up with her best friend. What if she'd lost her again, for good?!

Just then, Mira heard a familiar clap, and turned to see Miss Glitterhorn in the stableyard, standing next to Miss Hind, Darcy and Star.

'You didn't run away to live in the forest!' Mira shouted and flung herself at Darcy.

'Err, thank you, Mira,' said Miss Glitterhorn, and she clapped her hands again. 'Class Red, Darcy has something to say to you all.'

Darcy pushed Mira off (in a friendly way) and cleared her throat. With a solemn face, she said,

'I'm sorry that I have caused so much trouble. I only wanted everyone to have a completely and utterly amazing disco. I explained to Miss Glitterhorn that everything was all my fault – I took the Glitter Slime from the caves and I'm the one who disobeyed the quest orders.'

Star snorted as if she was apologising too.

Darcy looked around at Class Red. 'I said to Miss Glitterhorn that I don't think you should all be punished for something I did.'

Miss Glitterhorn nodded her head. 'Darcy has done the right thing and taken full responsibility for the Glitter Slime incident. Therefore I am pleased to say that the rest of Class Red SHALL go to the disco!'

Class Red cheered loudly, but Mira and Raheem didn't feel like cheering.

Freya ran over to give Darcy a thank you hug, and soon everyone followed. Even Jake gave Darcy a high five. Then he and Pegasus break-danced back to the stables.

Flo sniffed and wiped her nose on her sleeve. 'But it's just so sad you can't come to the disco too!'

Darcy gave her another hug. 'It's fine. You and Sparkles are brilliant dancers, you lead the dance for me, okay?'

Once everyone had headed back to the dormitories, talking about what they were going to wear for the disco, Mira and Raheem went to join Darcy. Mira gave her a huge hug.

Raheem shook her hand. 'That was a really nice thing you did,' he said.

Darcy shrugged, but she had tears in her eyes. 'Thanks guys. Come on, Star, let's get you to bed. We've got a long day of picking up poo tomorrow in detention.'

Mira heard Dave give an 'I'm hungry' snort from his stable – she'd forgotten to get him his extra hay. 'Are you sure you're okay, Darcy? I can help you groom Star?'

'I'm fine.' Darcy sniffed. 'Dave needs you. We'll see you in the morning.'

Mira went to pick up more hay for Dave and watched Darcy wheel into Star's stable. She felt awful that Darcy couldn't go to the disco.

Even though Darcy *had* caused all the trouble, she'd only done it because she wanted the disco to be the best EVER. Mira just wished there was a way to help Darcy, without getting anyone else into trouble . . .

CHAPTER NINE
Friends Together

All lessons were cancelled the next morning,
so that everyone could get ready for the disco in
the afternoon. Darcy and Star were very quiet at
breakfast before they headed out to the stables
for their detention of picking up poo and stable
tidying.

No one was surprised when Jake announced
himself the new Chief Organiser of the Disco
Committee for last-minute preparations. But they
were surprised when he and Pegasus welcomed
them all into the hall with a tray of delicious-
looking pastries!

'I didn't know Jake was such a brilliant baker!' said Mira, scoffing a large chocolate éclair.

Raheem fed Brave a pain-au-chocolat. 'It turns out that Pegasus is half French,' he said.

'These are delicious!' cried Mira, through a mouthful of pastry. Dave ate five more éclairs and gave a happy fart.

Jake gave out party assignments to all the different pupils. Mira and Dave were sent to mix the fruit punch, then helped make the unicorn disco outfits. Jake had even prepared a pile of doughnuts for Dave to snack on, so he wouldn't cause too much chaos. Mira had to admit, when Jake channelled all his annoyingness into being in charge, he was actually pretty good at it.

Mira was just trying to squeeze Dave into his dancing jacket but he wouldn't stop wriggling. 'Hold still Dave!' she said. 'Do you want another doughnut? Oh, you've already finished them all.'

Dave snorted, and then looked pointedly out
of the window.

Mira saw where he was looking. Darcy and Star
were shovelling unicorn poo in the stableyard.

Mira looked around her. Everywhere she turned, pupils and unicorns were creating a magical disco room. Sparkly bunting was going up on the walls, twinkly lights crisscrossed the ceiling. And the treats table was looking spectacular. Darcy would love it.

Dave snuffled again and farted loudly.

'Okay, okay!' said Mira as she took off Dave's dancing jacket. 'I agree that Darcy is our friend and the disco won't be nearly as fun without her.'

Dave nodded and waggled his ears.

Mira thought for a moment. She thought of dancing in the kitchen with Pickles and Rani. They'd had so much fun, even though it was just the three of them ... WAIT A MINUTE!

Mira had an idea. But she needed the help of her friends.

Mira quickly whispered in Dave's ear and Dave trotted over to Brave. He and Raheem were helping to set up the speakers for the DJ.

Brave and Dave started snuffling at each other. Raheem left his speaker plugs and came over to ask Mira what was going on. She explained that the unicorns were going to create a diversion.

Raheem looked both confused and scared.

Just then Brave gave one of his thundering neighs, and when everyone turned to look at him, Dave kicked over a large speaker. This in turn banged into the treat table, knocking over a unicorn made from profiteroles that Jake and

Pegasus had been creating for several hours.

Miss Hind, who was overseeing the preparations, blew her whistle loudly and ran over to see what was going on as profiteroles rolled all over the floor. Mira quickly ducked down and grabbed a handful of treats from the table and a spare string of sparkly lights.

Jake went bright red and started stomping around and shouting, and while Miss Hind was calming him down, Mira whispered, 'Now's our chance!'

She picked up Darcy and Star's disco outfits from the rail and yanked Raheem out of the hall, with Dave and Brave following closely behind. Mira noticed that Dave had several profiteroles skewered on his horn and was throwing them up into the air and catching them in his mouth.

'What now?' asked Raheem as he stumbled out of the hall.

'We're going to see Darcy,' said Mira.

Raheem rolled his eyes and groaned. 'Mira, Darcy is in detention and it's all fine, and we're

preparing for the disco and it's all going to
be nice and calm with no more danger. Or
excitement.'

'No,' said Mira, marching them all off towards
the stables. 'We owe it to our friend to give her
the very best disco ever!'

UUU

'What are you doing here?' exclaimed Darcy.
She and Star were looking at pictures on Darcy's
phone.

'Darcy, you SHALL go to the disco!' said Mira
dramatically.

Darcy frowned. 'I can't go to the disco Mira,
I'll get in so much trouble!'

Mira grinned. 'Aha! Well if Darcy can't come

to the disco, then WE'LL bring the disco to Darcy!'

'Oh, okay!' said Darcy. She looked confused. 'Actually, I don't understand what's going on.'

'We're having our own disco. Just us!' cried Mira. 'And the theme is Glitter Fever.'

Darcy blinked in surprise.

'We've brought all the stuff,' continued Mira, giving Darcy a slightly squashed profiterole. 'There's just one thing we need.'

'A Chief Organiser,' said Raheem, handing Darcy a clipboard. 'The best party planner ever.'

Darcy stared at the clipboard, and then looked up at them. She frowned. Mira's heart sank.

'You guys . . .' Darcy said slowly. 'Had better

watch out. Because . . .'

Darcy spun around in her chair and pointed her finger at Mira and Raheem. 'GLITTER FEVER'S GONNA GET YOU!'

'YAY!' said Mira, and Raheem grinned (but he also pulled his T-shirt up over his mouth, just in case glitter fever *was* something that could make you poorly).

Darcy turned back to Mira. 'So where *is* our disco?'

'The dorm,' Mira said with a great big grin. 'But first, we need to make an epic glitterball.'

Darcy squealed with delight and the three friends quickly set about gathering as much glitter and sparkle as they could find. Darcy had stashed away the small glitterball from earlier and Star sorted as much glittery unicorn poo from their muck pile as possible.

Mira got all the boiler suits out of the laundry basket and shook the glitter dust off them. Raheem even went and got all the hand-mirrors from the unicorn grooming store.

'Right, let's make this into a glitterball!' said Mira.

When they'd finished, Darcy wiped her hands on her trousers, then wiped a tear from her eye. 'It's beautiful,' she said. 'You guys are the best friends ever. And this is going to be the best DISCO ever!'

'Even though it's just us,' said Raheem.

'Especially because it's just us,' smiled Mira as she pulled her best friends into a big hug.

CHAPTER TEN

Dave Does Disco!

The lunch bell rang, and Mira nodded to her friends. 'Quick! Before anyone sees us!' she said.

Dave's tummy rumbled.

'Are you okay?' she asked him. Dave nodded. Today, friendship meant more than anything – even lunch.

They worked as a team. Dave, Star and Brave rolled the glitterball from the stableyard up into the Class Red dorm. Mira and Raheem followed them with brooms, sweeping up the glittery, pooey trail they left behind them.

Darcy supervised and gave instructions.

They hid the glitterball behind one of the Class Red dorm curtains and ran down to the canteen.

'Where did you guys get to?' said Jake as they sat down at the Class Red table with their trays. There were smears of chocolate on his face and he looked a bit frazzled.

'Oh, we were just . . . around!' replied Mira, trying to look calm. She was still pretty sweaty and a bit stinky from creating the glitterball. 'We were making . . . something. Actually, I really wanted your opinion on a recipe for croissants . . .'

Mira knew that asking Jake for advice would distract him. Soon everyone was chatting about how excited they were for the disco (apart from Jake who was still going on about croissants).

The lunch bell rang again and there was a stampede of pupils and unicorns running to the disco. Whoops and cheers came from the hall and then music started blaring out.

'Are you sure you don't mind missing it?' asked Darcy quietly.

Mira gave her a huge hug. 'Are you kidding?' she said cheerfully. 'Let's go and have our own dorm disco!'

ᑌᑌᑌ

Back in the Class Red dormitory, Raheem put on some music and moved all the bedside lamps to shine on the glitterball. He put the glitterball on a record player on a bedside table so it would

spin and send sparkly light all over the walls.

They all got changed into their disco outfits

and Darcy had the idea of taking down one of

the red curtains to make a red carpet. Then they

took turns pretending to arrive in style with

their unicorns.

They were dancing around and singing

at the top of their voices, so didn't hear the

door bang. So they were quite surprised when

they did hear the

SSRREEEEECHHH

of Miss Hind's whistle.

'WHAT are you DOING in here?!' the PE
teacher yelled at them.

Mira noticed that Miss Hind wasn't wearing her
usual sportswear. Instead she was wearing a white,
shiny disco dress and she'd even done her hair in
a swishy ponytail instead of a scraped-back bun.

'You look lovely, Miss Hind!' said Darcy.

Raheem sank down on the bed, his head in
his hands. 'I knew it! We're in even more trouble.
We'll be banned from Unicorn School for ever.
Expelled! Sent to prison!'

Miss Hind pointed at them all in turn. 'Darcy,
YOU should be in detention. Mira, YOU should
be at the disco and Raheem YOU should be
in the lighting booth and – WHAT IS THAT

BEAUTIFUL THING?!'

The three friends followed Miss Hind's finger

which was now pointing at their glitterball.

Darcy stepped in to defend her friends. 'It's a glitterball, Miss Hind. Again, this is all my fault. Mira and Raheem didn't want me to feel left out so they made me a disco in the dorm. Please, let them go back to the disco. I'll go back to detention. I'm sorry!'

Mira was shocked to hear Darcy saying it was her fault, when the dorm disco had been Mira's idea! She started to explain that to Miss Hind, but the teacher's face was now doing funny things. Her eyebrows looked cross, her cheeks were bright red and her mouth was trying really hard not to smile.

'Grrrr,' Miss Hind growled. 'This is all extremely frustrating. Although NONE of you are where you should be, you have behaved in a

way which promotes the Unicorn School values

of friendship and loyalty. We will ALL discuss this

with Madame Shetland. Follow me.'

Miss Hind stomped off, then turned back. 'And

bring that glorious glitterball with you.'

The three friends exchanged glances. What was

going to happen next . . .?

They picked up the glitterball and raced

through the corridors to stand outside the hall.

Mira could see it did look truly spectacular and

was full of their friends and the other Unicorn

School pupils having fun. Miss Hind was waiting

at the door with Madame Shetland. They

both looked very stern, despite their glittering,

glamorous disco clothes. Miss Hind was still red in the face as she explained what a nice thing Mira and Raheem did for their friend.

Madame Shetland nodded and crossed her arms. 'Darcy, you deserved your detention. But taking responsibility so that all your classmates could go to the disco was the right thing to do. Have you learned your lesson?'

Darcy nodded.

'And Mira and Raheem,' Madame Shetland continued. 'You have taken rather a lot of risks these last few days, but it has been to help and support your friend.'

Mira and Raheem nodded. Mira crossed her fingers behind her back.

Madame Shetland finally smiled. 'Therefore you have definitely adhered to Unicorn School Rule no 64: Being a Loyal Friend Overrides Other Behaviour On Certain Occasions. And, as such . . . You shall ALL go to the disco!'

'HOOORAAAAAY!' Mira and Darcy were yelling and high fiving. Raheem was a bit quiet.

Miss Hind tapped him on the shoulder. 'Hurry up, Raheem, they need you in the lighting booth. And set up that glitterball right away.'

Raheem grinned happily and trotted off with Brave.

When Mira and Darcy went into the hall, the whole of Class Red bundled on top of them, cheering loudly.

By the time Mira and Darcy had finished
hugging everyone, Raheem had set up the
glitterball. Then he switched on the lights.

The entire hall was lit with squillions of magical sparkles, as if the stars had come down from the sky and were shining just for the disco.

Just then *Glitter Fever's Gonna Get You* came on the speakers, the crowd split and Class Red ran on to the dance floor in two straight lines, children in front of unicorns.

'My routine!' Darcy squeaked.

Freya gave her a friendly punch on the shoulder and shouted over the music, 'We've been practising!' Then she ran to join Princess and her friends in the dance. As the lines parted with each partner doing their very best jazz hands or hooves, Darcy launched herself right down the centre, doing an endless spinning wheelie.

Mira laughed and felt a nudge. Dave was holding out a hoof. She giggled again and curtsied to him. 'Why, yes, I will have this dance, thank you!' They had to dodge Rani and Angelica who were doing the most incredible series of spinning lifts right across the hall. They looked so cool that people in their path stopped dancing to applaud them. Mira had never seen her sister look happier. She gave her a big thumbs-up.

Freya shimmied over to Mira and did a spin. She sniffed and made a funny face. Over the loud music,

Freya shouted into Mira's ear, 'Does something smell weird?'

A small clump of hay coated in glittery unicorn poo fell off the glitterball on to Princess, and Mira quickly shouted back, 'Let's go and get some punch!'

They danced over to the treats table and helped themselves to some rainbow cake and marshmallows dipped in melted chocolate. Flo asked Darcy if she liked the party.

'Well,' Darcy said thoughtfully, 'you've not quite got the bunting right, and the line dancing wasn't really – OW!'

Mira had poked Darcy in the ribs.

Darcy cleared her throat. 'I mean,' she said, 'it's totally perfect. Come on, let's dance!'

They all pranced back on to the dancefloor in their pairs. Dave slipped on a bit of glitterball poo and managed to do the partner slide with jazz hooves that he'd found so hard in rehearsal!

Mira laughed and spun round her unicorn. It had been a very eventful few days at Unicorn School. But now she was disco dancing with Dave and all of her best friends. It was . . .

AMAZING!

DAZZLING DISCO QUIZ

How much have YOU remembered about *The Naughtiest Unicorn and the School Disco*?

1. What's the name of Mira and Rani's cat?
    a. Pom Pom
    b. Poppy
    c. Pickles

2. What's the first super special treat Mira brings for Dave in this book?
    a. Cream cake
    b. Jammy dodger
    c. Strawberry lace

3. What's the theme of the Unicorn School Disco?
    a. Glitz and Glamour
    b. Gardens
    c. Glitter Fever

4. Who is quest leader in this book?
   a. Flo
   b. Freya
   c. Jake

5. Raheem insists Brave wears this when they go into the Crystal Maze mine…
   a. Protective face mask
   b. High visibility jacket
   c. Safety helmet

6. What is School Rule Number 73?
   a. Always Be kind To Your Unicorn
   b. Give Dave Plenty Of Doughnuts
   c. Leave The Forest As You Find It

Answers:

Mostly As: Good effort but no prize this time!

Mostly Bs: Not quite! Why not read the book again and then see how many questions you get right?

Mostly Cs: Whoop! You are the star of the show and the top of the class. Well done!

UNICORN JOKES

What did the mirror say to the unicorn?
I see u-nicorn

Which unicorn always gets forgotten?
The who-nicorn

Why did the skeleton not go to the disco?
Because he had no body to go with!

Where do unicorns throw their rubbish?
The glitter bin

What happened to the smallest unicorn?
He grew-nicorn

What dance would a car do at the disco?
Brake dance

Which unicorn is a ghost in disguise?
The Woooooo-nicorn!

Catch up on all of Mira and Dave's adventures at Unicorn School!

EGMONT

THE NAUGHTIEST UNICORN
AT CHRISTMAS

snow, ho ho!

PIP BIRD

ILLUSTRATED BY DAVID O'CONNELL

Coming soon

Unicorn School is *SNOW* much fun!

EGMONT

AMELIA FANG

Join the little
vampire with a big heart
for some howlingly hilarious adventures!

Sink your fangs into the new

AMELIA FANG

adventures

AMELIA FANG and the LOST YETI TREASURES

LAURA ELLEN ANDERSON

AMELIA FANG and the NAUGHTY CATICORNS

LAURA ELLEN ANDERSON

COMING SOON!